For my
darling Amy
A.D.

For
Julie Chalmers
S.H.

First U.S. edition 1995

Library of Congress Cataloging-in-Publication Data

Durant, Alan.
Mouse party / by Alan Durant ; illustrated by Sue Heap.—1st U.S. ed.
Summary: A mouse moves into a deserted house and invites all his
friends to a party, only to be surprised by an unexpected arrival.
ISBN 1-56402-584-5 (hardcover)—ISBN 1-56402-585-3 (paperback)
[1. Animals—Fiction.   2. Parties—Fiction.   3. Dwellings—Fiction.]
I. Heap, Sue, 1954 — ill.   II. Title.
PZ7.D9317Mo   1995
[E]—dc20   94-38904

10 9 8 7 6 5 4 3 2 1

Printed in Italy

This book was typeset in Providence-Sans.

The pictures in this book were done in pen and ink and watercolor.

Candlewick Press
2067 Massachusetts Avenue
Cambridge, Massachusetts 02140

Alan Durant

MOUSE PARTY

illustrated by
Sue Heap

CANDLEWICK PRESS
CAMBRIDGE, MASSACHUSETTS

Mouse found a deserted house and decided to make his home there. But it was a very big house for such a small mouse and he felt a little lonely. *I know*, he thought, *I'll have a party.* So he sent invitations to all his friends.

The first
to arrive were

Cat with a **mat** and

Dog with a **log**.

Then came **Hare** with a **chair**,

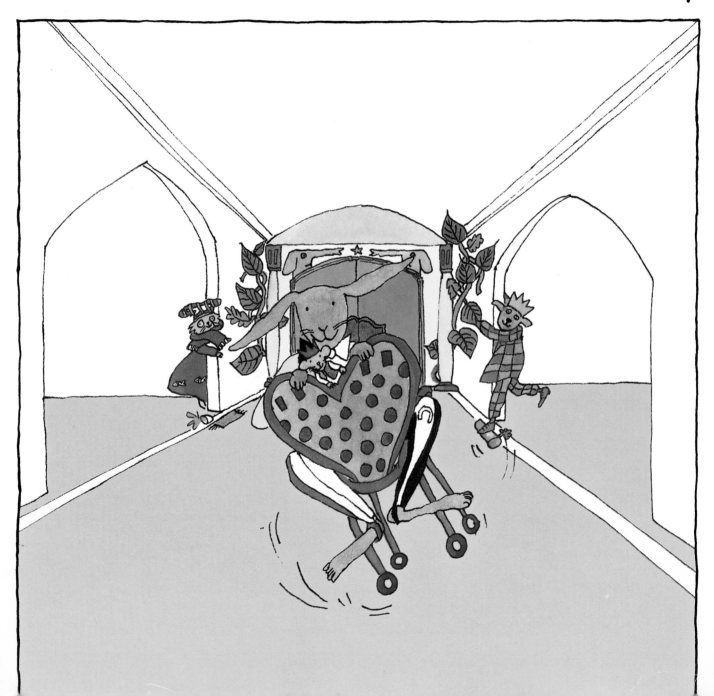

Owl with a **towel**,

Giraffe with a **bath,**

Hen with a **pen**,

Lamb with some jam,

Rat with a **bat** in a **hat**,

and **Fox** with a **box** full of **lots**

and colors of **socks**.

and **lots** of different kinds

"Let's party!" said Mouse.   But...

Rat- a-

tat - tat!

It was an elephant with two trunks.
He was blowing through one and
carrying the other.
"Hello," said Mouse. "Welcome to my house."

"*Your* house?" said the elephant,
and he looked quite angry.
"I've just been away on a long vacation.
This house, I must tell you, is mine!"

"Oh," said Mouse, Lamb, Hare, Rat, and Bat.

"Oh," said Hen, Dog, Owl, Fox, and Giraffe.

But, "Come in, come in!" said Cat.
"You're just in time for the party."

"A party . . . for me?" said Elephant.
"Oh, my! Yippee!"

So they drank and they ate and they danced

until late and had the most marvelous party.

And later, when the guests had
all gone home, leaving Elephant
and Mouse alone, Elephant said,
"I think, little Mouse, perhaps
it's true, there's room for us
both in this house, don't you?"

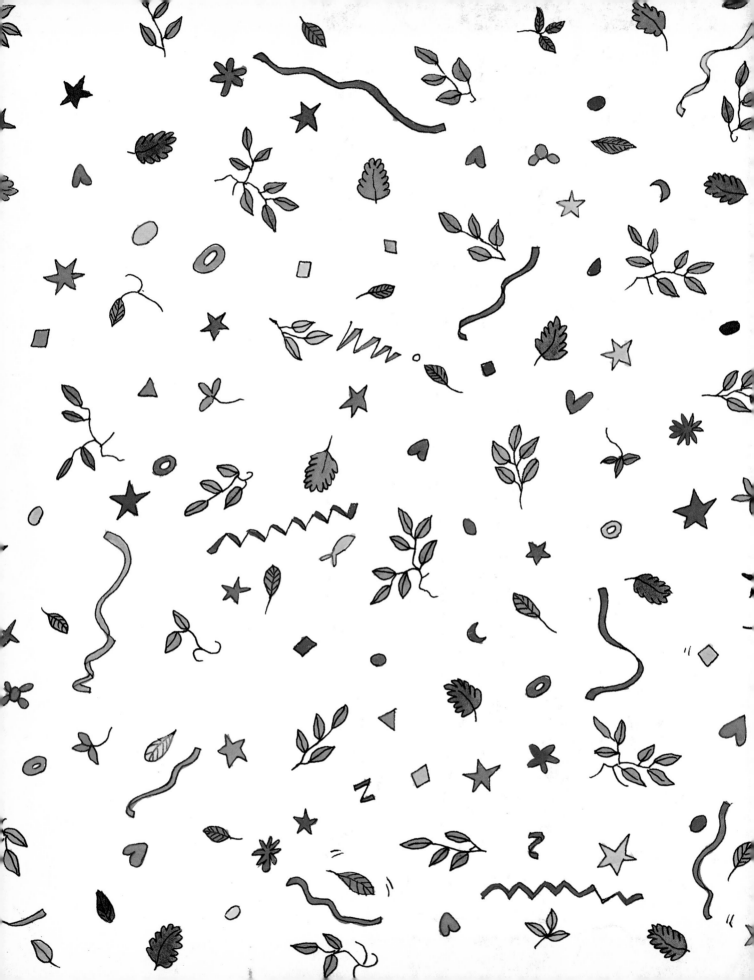